THE LEGO NINJAGO MOVIE

LORD GARMADON, EVIL DAD

ADAPTED BY MICHAEL PETRANEK
FROM THE SCREENPLAY

STORY BY HILARY WINSTON &
BOB LOGAN & PAUL FISHER AND
BOB LOGAN & PAUL FISHER &
WILLIAM WHEELER & TOM WHEELER

SCREENPLAY BY BOB LOGAN &
PAUL FISHER & WILLIAM WHEELER &
TOM WHEELER AND JARED STERN &
JOHN WHITTINGTON

SCHOLASTIC INC.

Adapted by Michael Petranek from the screenplay

Story by Hilary Winston & Bob Logan & Paul Fisher and Bob Logan &
Paul Fisher & William Wheeler & Tom Wheeler

Screenplay by Bob Logan & Paul Fisher & William Wheeler &
Tom Wheeler and Jared Stern & John Whittington

ISBN 978-1-338-21445-1

10 9 8 7 6 5 4 3 2 1   17 18 19 20 21
Printed in the U.S.A.   40

First printing 2017
Book design by Jessica Meltzer

Hey there. Garmadon checking in. Lord Garmadon, that is. I've got four arms and pointy teeth, and I'm pretty much all about conquering Ninjago City. It's been a dream of mine for a while. And I'm pretty close to achieving it. But first, here's more about me . . .

So like I said, I'm a bad guy . . . but not just any bad guy. I've been called the baddest guy ever in the history of Ninjago City.

Whoa, look at me! I look cool. Not bad!

I've got a son, but he's not evil like his old man. La-Lloyd is his name. I just learned that he's also the leader of the Secret Ninja Force. I've been fighting the Green Ninja for a while now — never knew he was my kid!

More on that later . . .

This is me and La-Lloyd's mom, Koko. There was a time when I wasn't so evil. Koko and I were together before I decided to just go for the whole evil lord thing.

Koko likes to tell people I tried doing an office job for a while, but it wasn't the right fit. So I decided to be a full-time bad guy.

Did my family support me? No. You see, I've got a brother named Master Wu, and he trains that Secret Ninja Force.

If you've got a brother or a sister who won't share toys with you, trust me, it could be worse. My brother trains a group of high school kids to fight me! I mean, what's up with that?!

So yeah, the Secret Ninja Force. They're a bunch of high school kids who don't want me to have any fun or conquer Ninjago City. The Green Ninja is their leader.

My brother may have his own team of ninja, but I've got something even better — a Shark Army! Take that, ninja nerds!

We've got cool vehicles, too. Crabs, birds, you name it. We can crawl, fly, or swim right into your city.

That's just what we did during our most recent adventure . . .

All those mechs and awesome shark costumes came in handy when I decided to attack Ninjago City for the millionth time. It just never gets old to me! We started by flying into the city . . .

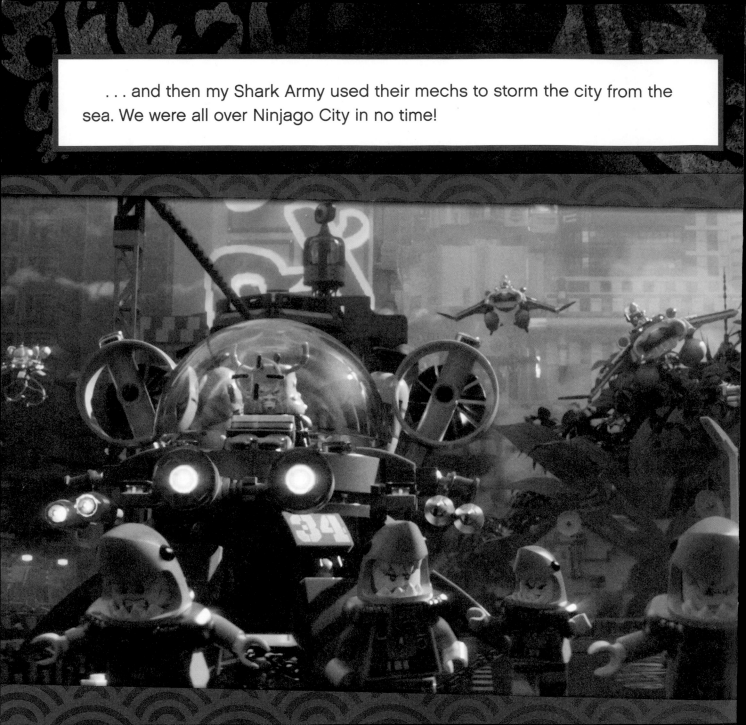

. . . and then my Shark Army used their mechs to storm the city from the sea. We were all over Ninjago City in no time!

The people were pretty stunned. See that hot dog guy? Stunned.
That's what happens when the most evil guy of all time takes over your city in less time than it takes to put mustard on a frank.

I was enjoying watching my Shark Army petrify all the people in the city. But suddenly, things started to be not so fun. I heard a lot of noise — and it was way louder than the usual noise of taking over the city.

It was the Secret Ninja Force! And they had vehicles, too! Big mechs. That wasn't good news for us. Still, we kept on fighting.

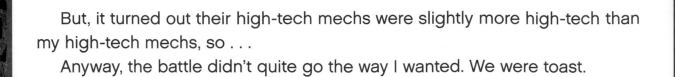

But, it turned out their high-tech mechs were slightly more high-tech than my high-tech mechs, so . . .

Anyway, the battle didn't quite go the way I wanted. We were toast.

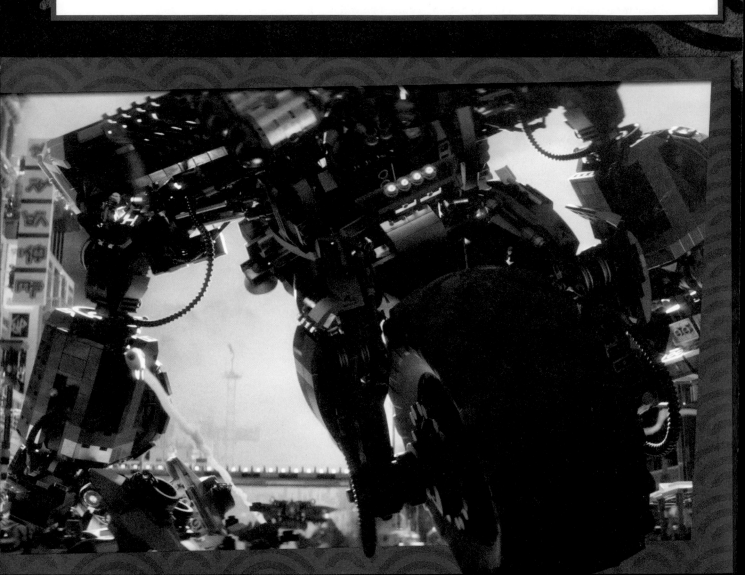

I stared down the Secret Ninja Force.

"I'll be back," I said. "And you better be ready for me to conquer Ninjago City!"

That's when the Green Ninja spoke up. "Oh, I'll be waiting . . . Dad . . ."

I couldn't believe it! It was La-Lloyd!

"That's right. It's me, your son. And it's *Lloyd*," he said. "You ruined my life, Dad."

"Pfft. No, it's L-L-O-Y-D — La-Lloyd. I named you," I said. "And that's not true — I haven't even been a *part* of your life. How could I ruin it? I wasn't even there."

We turned and headed back to our lair.

I couldn't believe my kid was the Green Ninja. I needed some serious "me" time. I had to think about what I should do next . . .

I guess I must have put my phone in my back pocket, because suddenly, I heard a voice talking to me.

"Hello?" I asked. "Who's this?"

I heard a tired voice on the other end. "It's Lloyd. Your son."

"La-Lloyd?" I asked. "I must have butt-dialed you."

I hung up. I needed to think of new ways to defeat the Secret Ninja Force, not spend time on the phone with my kid!

But it was good to know I had his phone number.

The Secret Ninja Force members are probably training, getting ready for me to come back. I mean, hey, I always come back! I love destroying stuff with my crazy machines.

So now that I know my kid's the Green Ninja, I need a new plan to conquer Ninjago City. I've got to put my kid in his place. I mean, I might be an evil warlord, but I'm still his dad!

And Daddy's got a plan that La-Lloyd will never see coming. Ha, ha, ha!